· AARON BLABEY ·

the BAD GUYS

GUIDE TO BEING GOOD

SCHOLASTIC INC.

· CHAPTER 1 ·
A NEW RECRUIT

Hey there, Mr. Wolf!

Say someone wanted to stop being seen as a
Bad Guy and join your **GOOD GUYS CLUB** . . .
. . . how would he go about it?

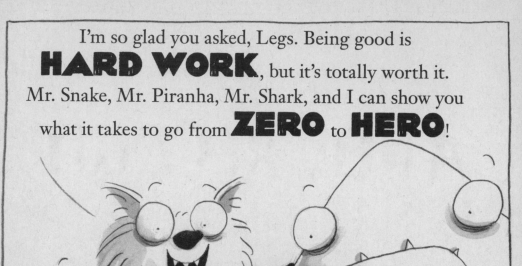

I'm so glad you asked, Legs. Being good is **HARD WORK**, but it's totally worth it. Mr. Snake, Mr. Piranha, Mr. Shark, and I can show you what it takes to go from **ZERO** to **HERO**!

Score! I'm getting tired of being known for scaring everyone. I've been branded a **DANGEROUS MONSTER** all over the internet . . . and it hurts.

DANGERO
DO NOT
APPROAC

Well, never fear my little eight-legged pal.

If you think you have what it takes,
I'll let you in on all our tricks.

Are you sure
you're
QUALIFIED,
man?

I mean, you don't exactly have the greatest track record.

Yeah, *hermano*. What he said.

Excuse me?!? Who **BROKE** the dogs out of the pound? Who **SAVED** the chickens from that evil chicken farm? Who **RESCUED** that cute little kitten who was stuck up a tree?

WE DID, that's who!

You're so brave, Wolfie.

MUNCH!

NOW,

please don't be **alarmed**.

It's true,

snakes can be tricky, and they do tend to

swallow whatever they like.

BUT—luckily, they swallow things *whole*

and I happen to know a **gentle,**

harmless technique that'll fix this right up.

Excuse me for **one** moment . . .

I SAID . . .

WHERE'S

THE PIRANHA?!

Hey, *chico*.
What's cookin'?

CHAPTER 2

FRIENDS AND ENEMIES

Still think we're not qualified?

I never said **WE**, Wolf . . .

In any case, the first step to being a hero is being able to tell your friends from your enemies.

That sounds easy.

Easy, he says.

Easy like a sweet old granny who wants to **EAT** you?

Easy like an adorable kitten—oh, whoops, I mean a **ZOMBIE** kitten?

AAARRGHH!!!

That was actually pretty funny.

Sizing up a stranger is anything but easy.
Looks can be deceiving.

CUTE can be **NASTY**.
SCARY can be **NICE**.

It's what's on the inside that counts.

THE DOG POUND

NASTY GUARDS

INNOCENT INMATES

WHO DESERVES TO BE LOCKED UP?

YOU BE THE JUDGE.

Take Marmalade, an adorable guinea pig.

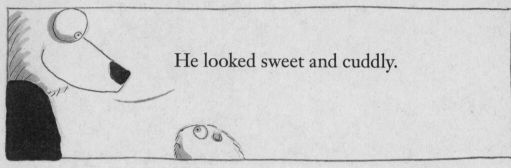

He looked sweet and cuddly.

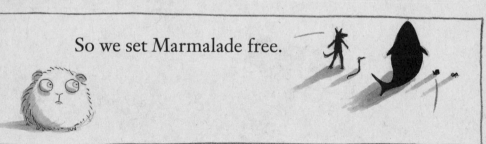

So we set Marmalade free.

SQUEAK!

That's

DOCTOR

Marmalade to you!

Yeah, he turned out
to be a billionaire
MAD SCIENTIST
who wants to take over
the world.

I **AM** a mad scientist!

I **DO** want to take
over the world!

So, not cute and cuddly at all.
Who'd have thought?

With the push of a button,
I'll turn every cute,
cuddly kitten into a

ZOMBIE!

HE HE HE
HE HE HE!

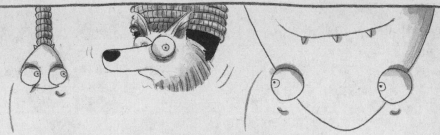

We *really* nailed
that one!

Good thing we had some help
stopping the zombie attack!

But our savior wasn't who we thought either.

FLING!

FLING!

Evil ninja with deadly moves?

Nope.

Well, sure. I DO have deadly moves.
I'm Agent Fox from the

INTERNATIONAL LEAGUE OF HEROES.

We're a secret global organization sworn to protect the earth from evil.

And that is what we do.

Hey! That's kind of what *we* do, isn't it, Wolfie?

Wolfie?

What's up with him?

. . . So awesome . . .
. . . so pretty . . .
. . . *guuuhhhhh* . . .
. . . *mhuuuunghhh* . . .

I'm not sure what's happening . . .

Never mind.

We thought she was evil.

But she turned out to be . . .
AMAZING.

I see. Don't judge a book by its cover.

So don't assume all furry eight-legged creatures are monsters. Right, Shark?

FAINT!

SPLAT!

He's working on it.

• CHAPTER 3 •
TICKET TO RIDE

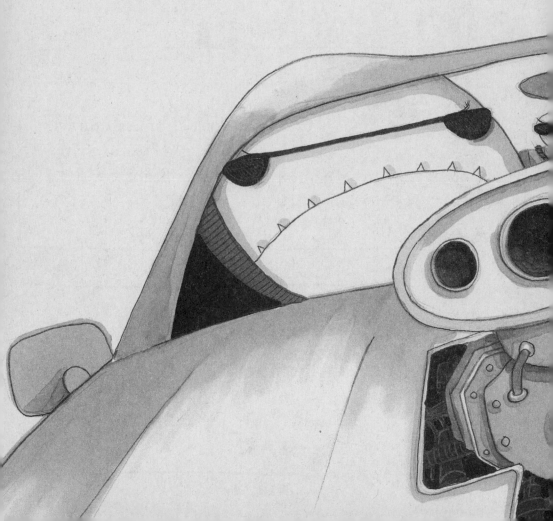

Heroes can be needed anywhere.
The right transportation is very important.

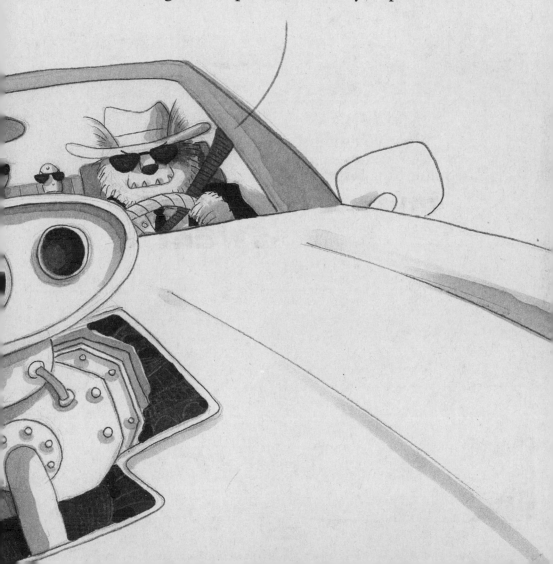

Now, you want something **FAST**.
Something **BOLD**. Something that says,
"**TRUST ME**. I know what I'm doing!"
Feast your eyes on this **SWEET** ride!

What about this rad motorcycle?

It's gotten me out of plenty of tough jams.

How tough?

It hauled you guys out of Marmalade's secret lair, didn't it?

When you're chasing a
ROCKET...

... you need something with extra
VROOM-VROOM
in its
BOOM-BOOM...

. . . like a

SUPERSONIC JET!

· CHAPTER 4 ·
MASTER OF DISGUISE

I should be the one to tell Legs about **DISGUISES**.

Hey! What's the Easter Bunny doing here? And where'd Mr. Shark go?

Relax. It's just me.

You are SO good at disguises.

Yeah. I know. I know all about—

Tell him they're **IMPORTANT**. That they help us go **UNNOTICED**. And fly **UNDER THE RADAR**.

OK.

Disguises are important.

They help us go unnoticed.

And fly under the radar.

All you need is a good costume and the perfect character. Right, Mindy?

You didn't see this, *chico*.

You hear me? This **NEVER** happened.

Disguises? Wicked vehicles?

Being good sounds so **AWESOME!**

Ah, that's **NOTHING**.

I can't believe you guys still haven't told him about

THE MOST IMPORTANT

part of being a hero . . .

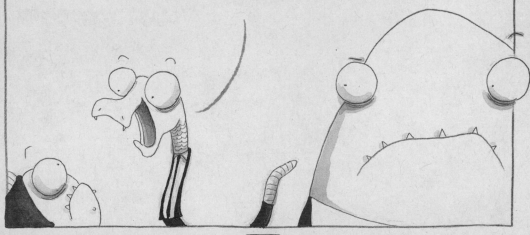

· CHAPTER 4 ½ ·
SNACKS

Being good takes a lot of energy. To stay strong, you have to keep your belly full.

It better not be full of fish, *hermano*.

I **LO-O-O-OVE** me some sushi.

We don't eat our friends!

Memorize this handy list of

APPROPRIATE

snack ideas.

BAD GUYS
NASTY TREATS

~~BATHERS~~

~~TOURISTS~~

~~INNOCENT BYSTANDERS~~

~~OLD LADIES~~

GOOD GUYS
HEALTHY CHOICES

FRUIT

VEGETABLES

TOFU

BREAD WITH WEIRD SEEDS AND STUFF IN IT

Ay, caramba!
You're no fun, man.

I'm **FUN**.
And tofu is **FUN**.

Why don't we stuff the Wolf with tofu,
and eat him? THAT'D be fun.

Uh . . . maybe we should
move on. What's next?

• CHAPTER 5 •
SURVIVAL SKILLS

I'm so glad you asked!

To be a real hero, you have to be **QUICK**, **NIMBLE**, and **LIGHT** on your feet.

Dangerous situations call for special skills that can only be mastered with practice.

Or, you know, you can just wing it.

If you need to break into a villain's office to hack their supercomputer . . .

. . . you'll need to be as **QUIET** as a mouse and as **GRACEFUL** as a swan.

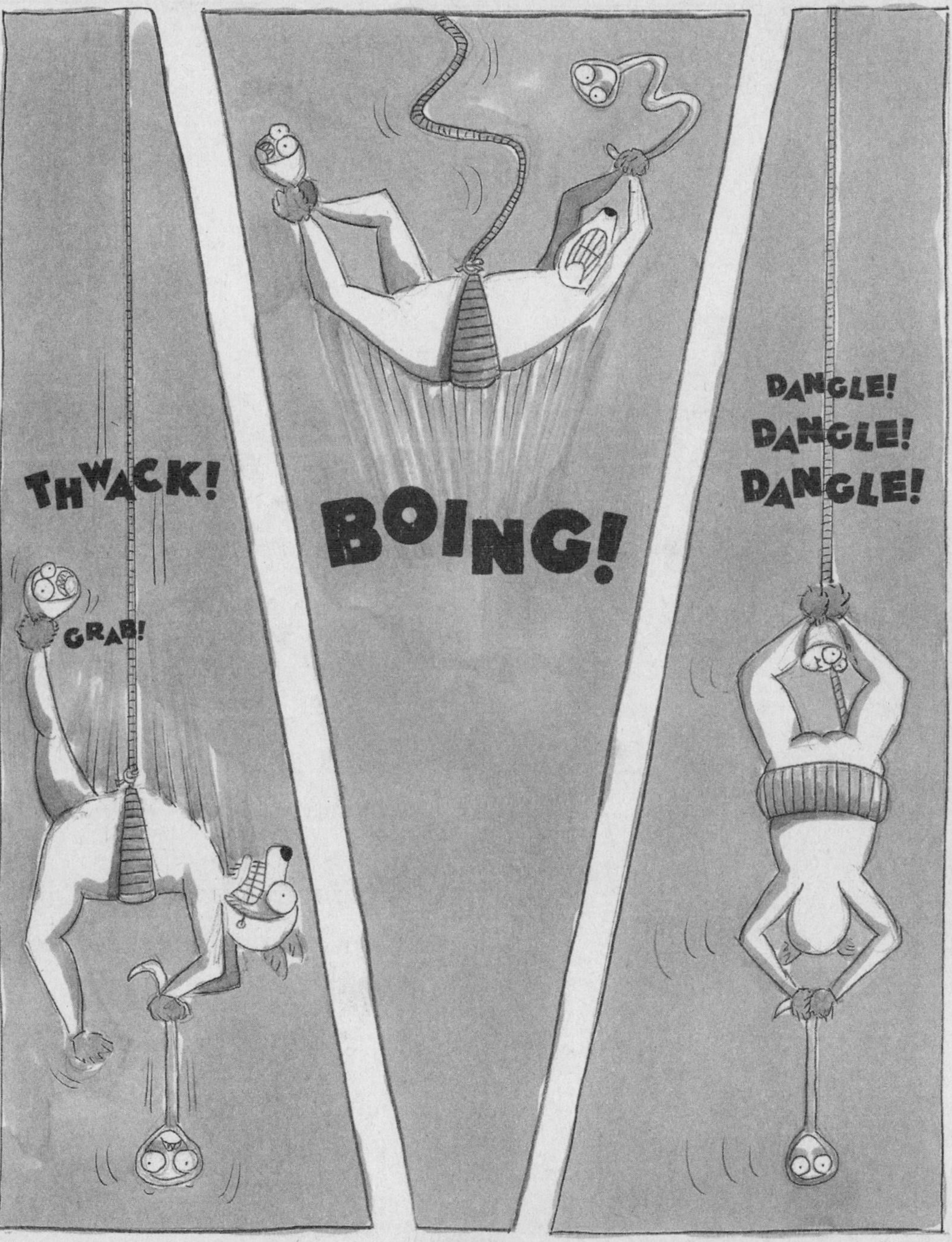
THWACK!
GRAB!
BOING!
DANGLE!
DANGLE!
DANGLE!

You really are very brave,
Mr. Wolf.

But remember, when you're
hanging, small movements can be

DANGEROUS,

so be as still as you can.

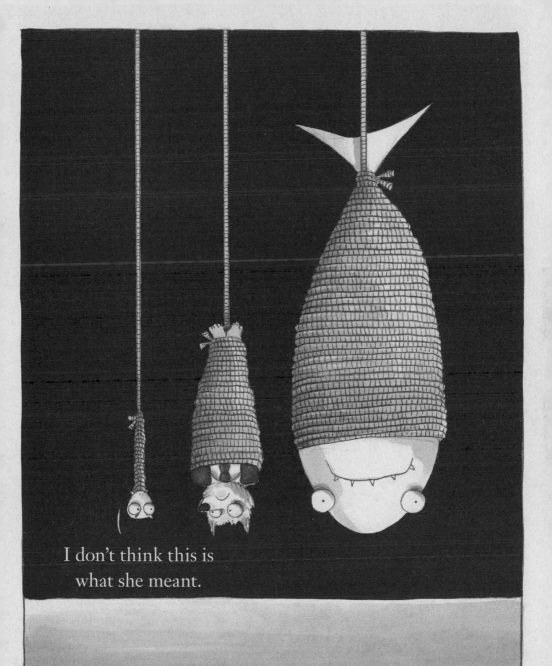

I don't think this is
what she meant.

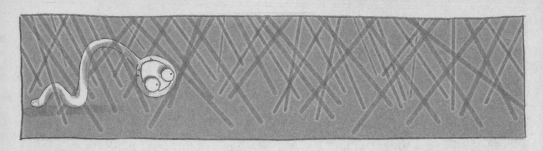

Laser beams are **SIZZLING** hot, so you have to be flexible to avoid them. Or send in a partner whose fur won't burn.

Hey!

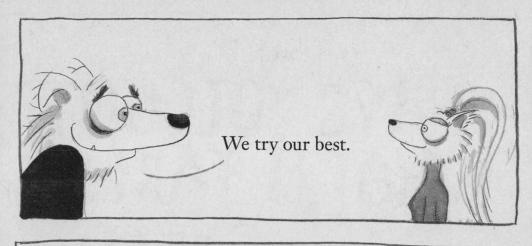

We try our best.

You're doing a good job.

You're . . .
almost . . .
professional.

He's a professional nutjob.

And lucky.

SO LUCKY.

It's the only reason that Wolf hasn't gotten us all killed!

· CHAPTER 6 ·
HAVE YOU GOT WHAT IT TAKES?

HA HA! HA HA! HA HA!

I know you don't mean that buddy.
It takes hard work and dedication
to be a **BAD GUY**.
Look at all of us!

Legs, do YOU have the right stuff to be a **BAD GUY**?

I know you only have eight tiny legs, but—

Legs? Who cares about legs? We don't need no stinkin' legs to get the job done.

What he said. Count me in.

That's what I like to hear.

What about YOU?

Yeah, I'm talking to you.

Think YOU have what it takes to join our team of **BAD GUYS** and do a little good around here?

YOUR NEXT MISSION?

CATCH UP ON ALL THE TROUBLE THE BAD GUYS GET INTO!